Storybreakers

Storybreakers Presents:

Lil' Lukie

Incredible illustrations, colours and lettering by Ger Hankey

www.lillukie.com

 @Storybreakers   Facebook.com/storybreakers

FOR _____

INSPIRED BY TRUE
EVENTS...

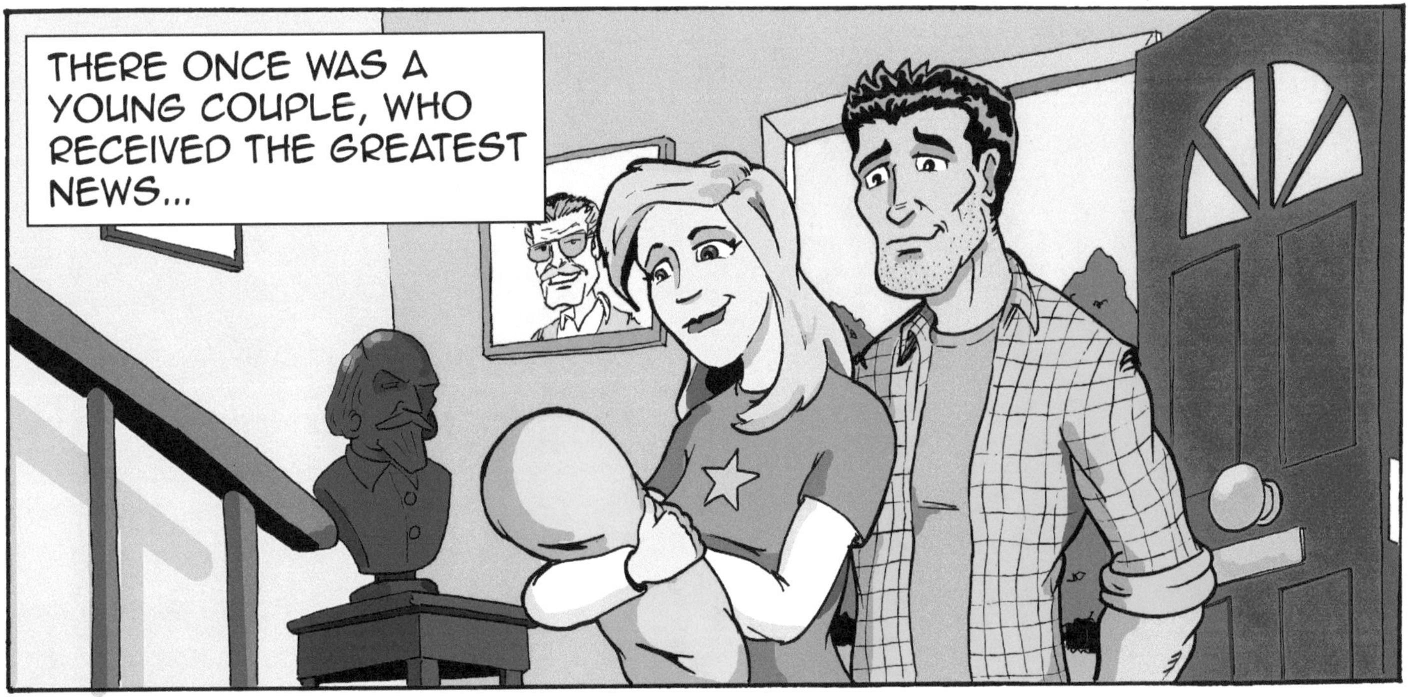
THERE ONCE WAS A YOUNG COUPLE, WHO RECEIVED THE GREATEST NEWS...

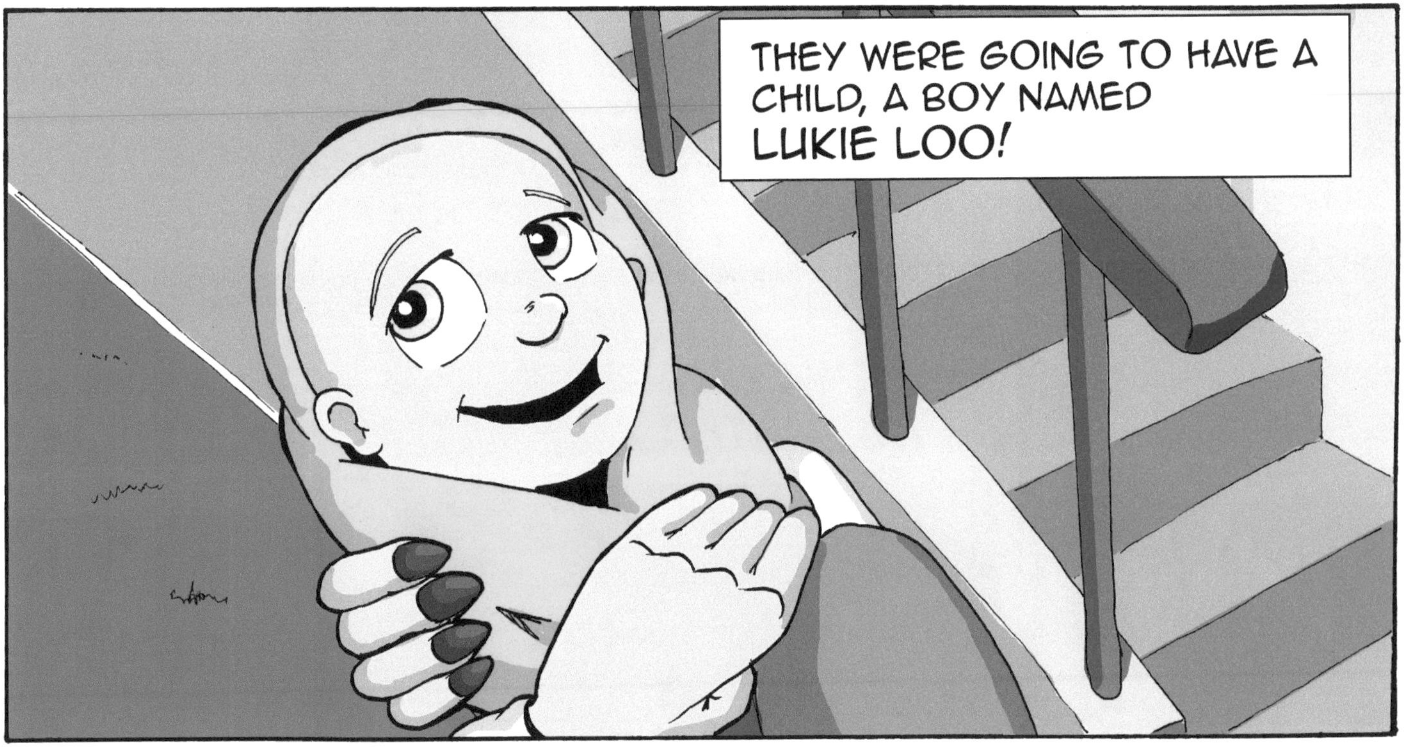
THEY WERE GOING TO HAVE A CHILD, A BOY NAMED LUKIE LOO!

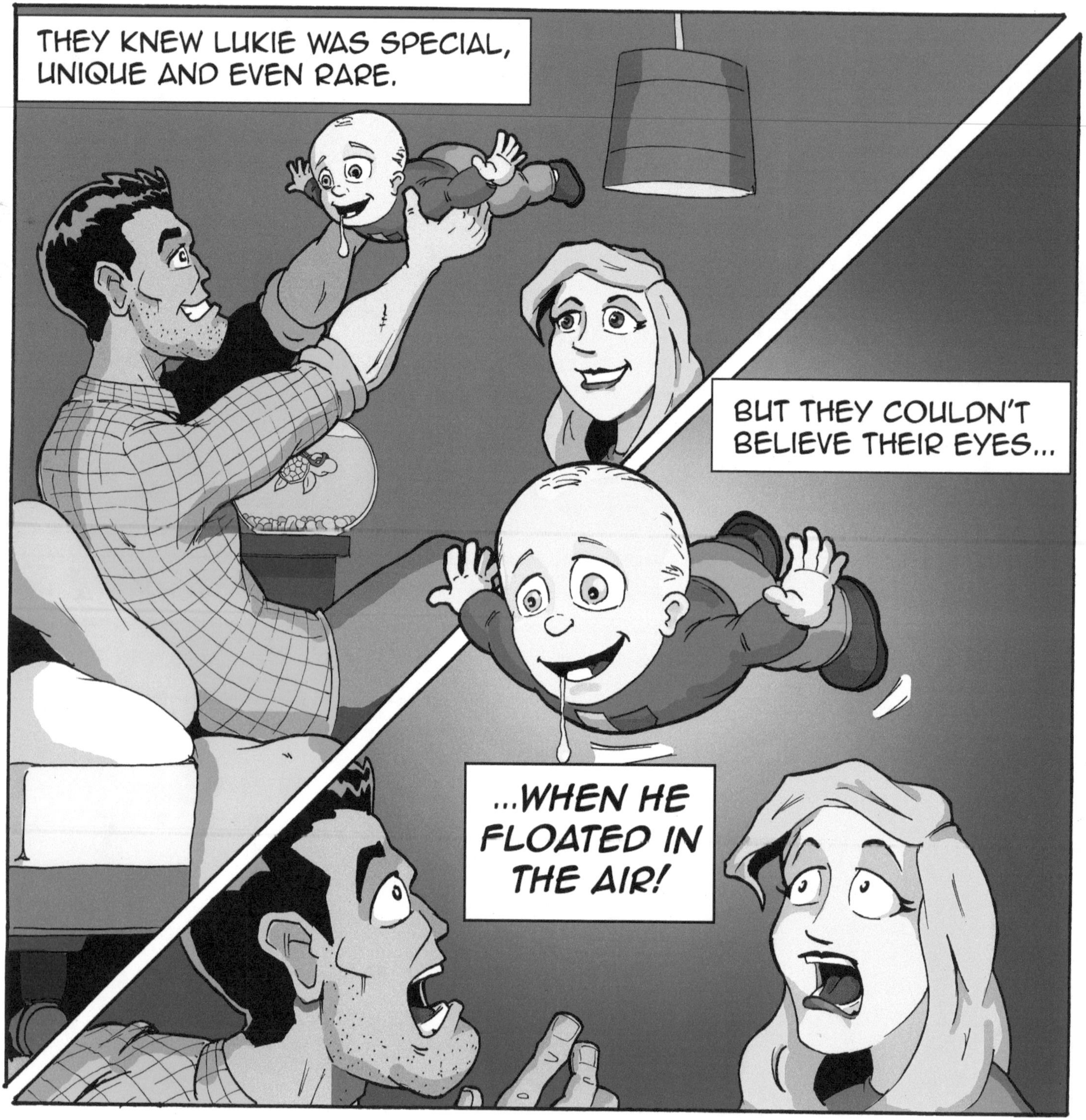
THEY KNEW LUKIE WAS SPECIAL, UNIQUE AND EVEN RARE.
BUT THEY COULDN'T BELIEVE THEIR EYES...
...WHEN HE FLOATED IN THE AIR!

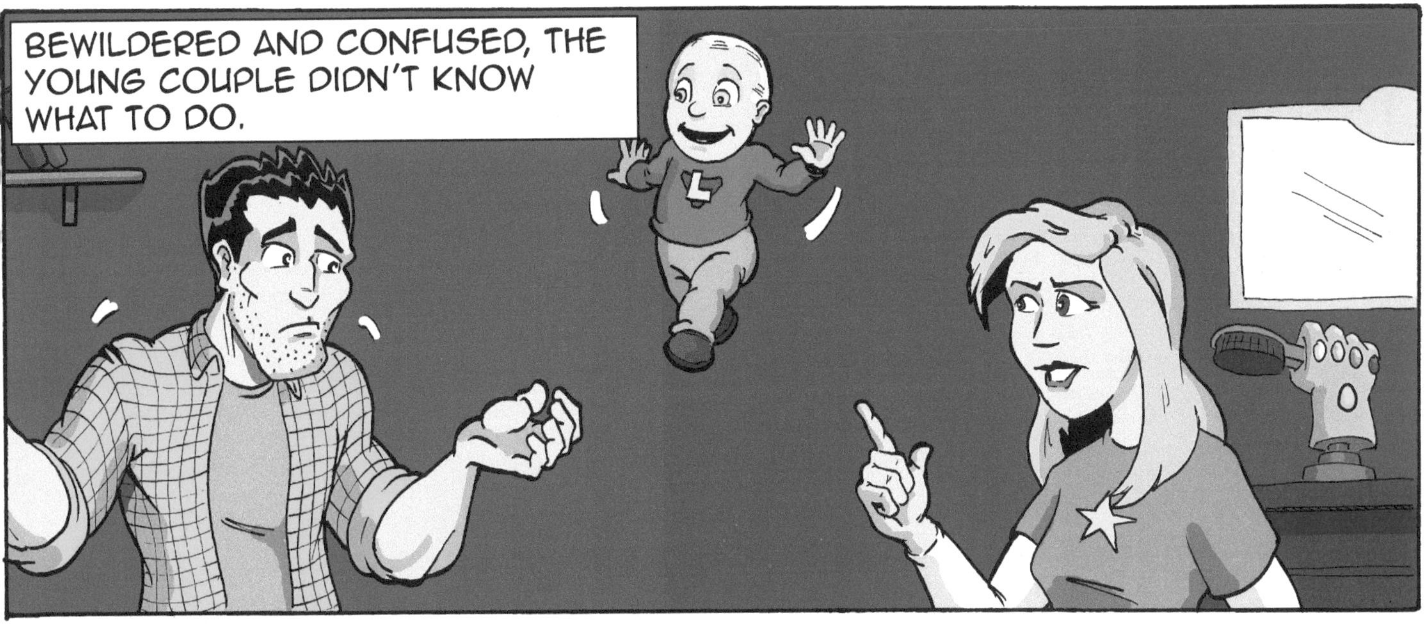
BEWILDERED AND CONFUSED, THE YOUNG COUPLE DIDN'T KNOW WHAT TO DO.

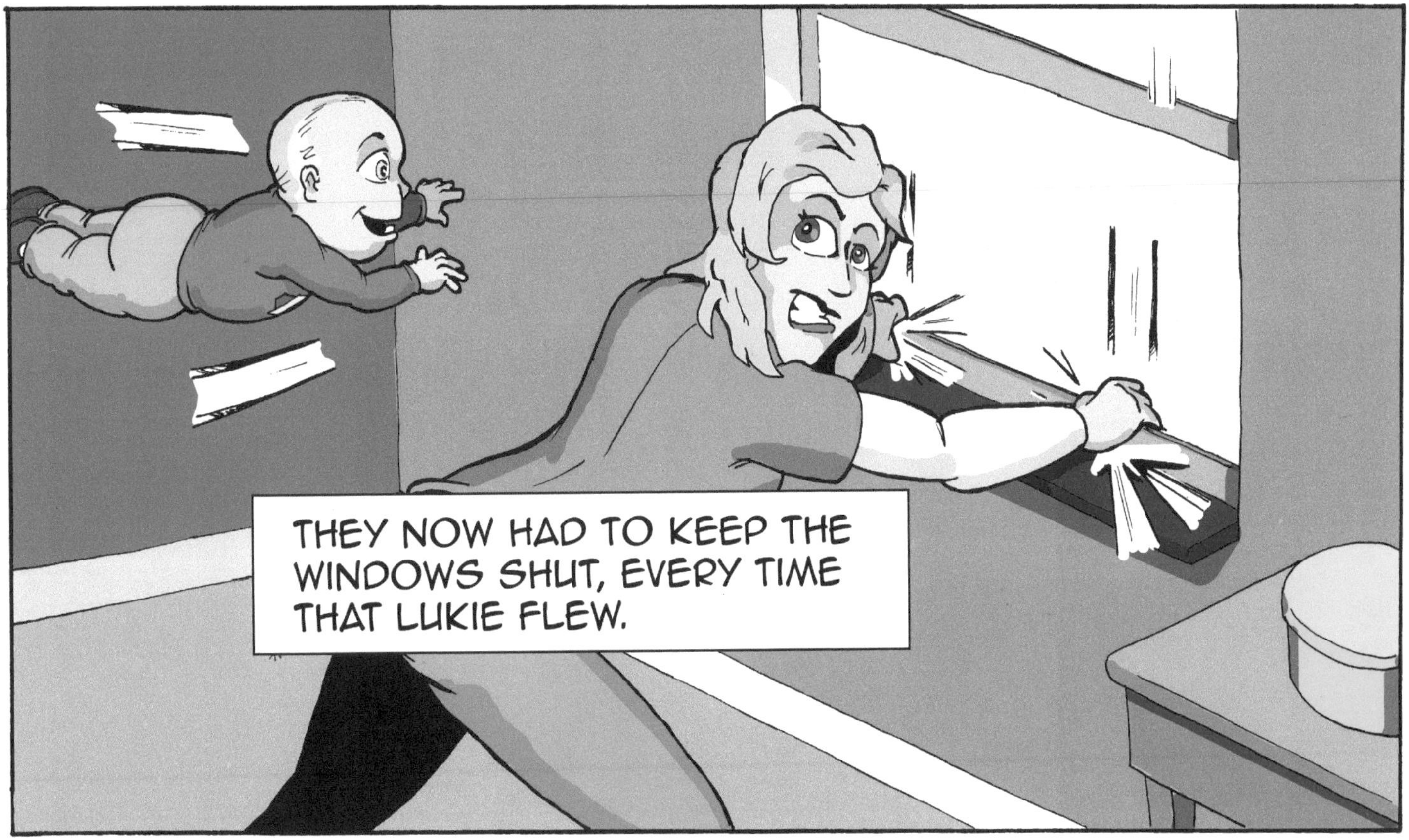
THEY NOW HAD TO KEEP THE WINDOWS SHUT, EVERY TIME THAT LUKIE FLEW.

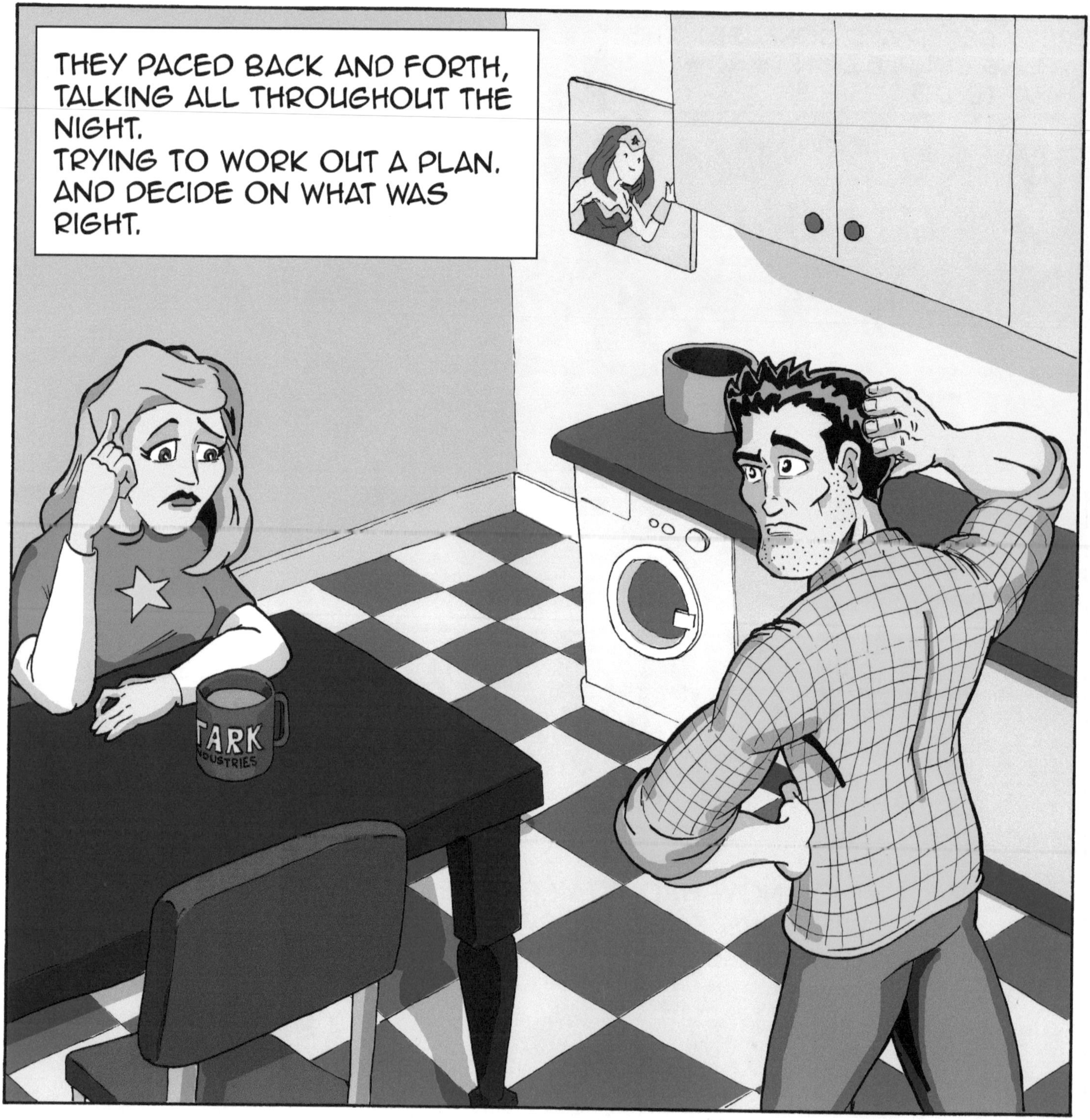
THEY PACED BACK AND FORTH, TALKING ALL THROUGHOUT THE NIGHT.
TRYING TO WORK OUT A PLAN. AND DECIDE ON WHAT WAS RIGHT.
TARK
NDUSTRIES

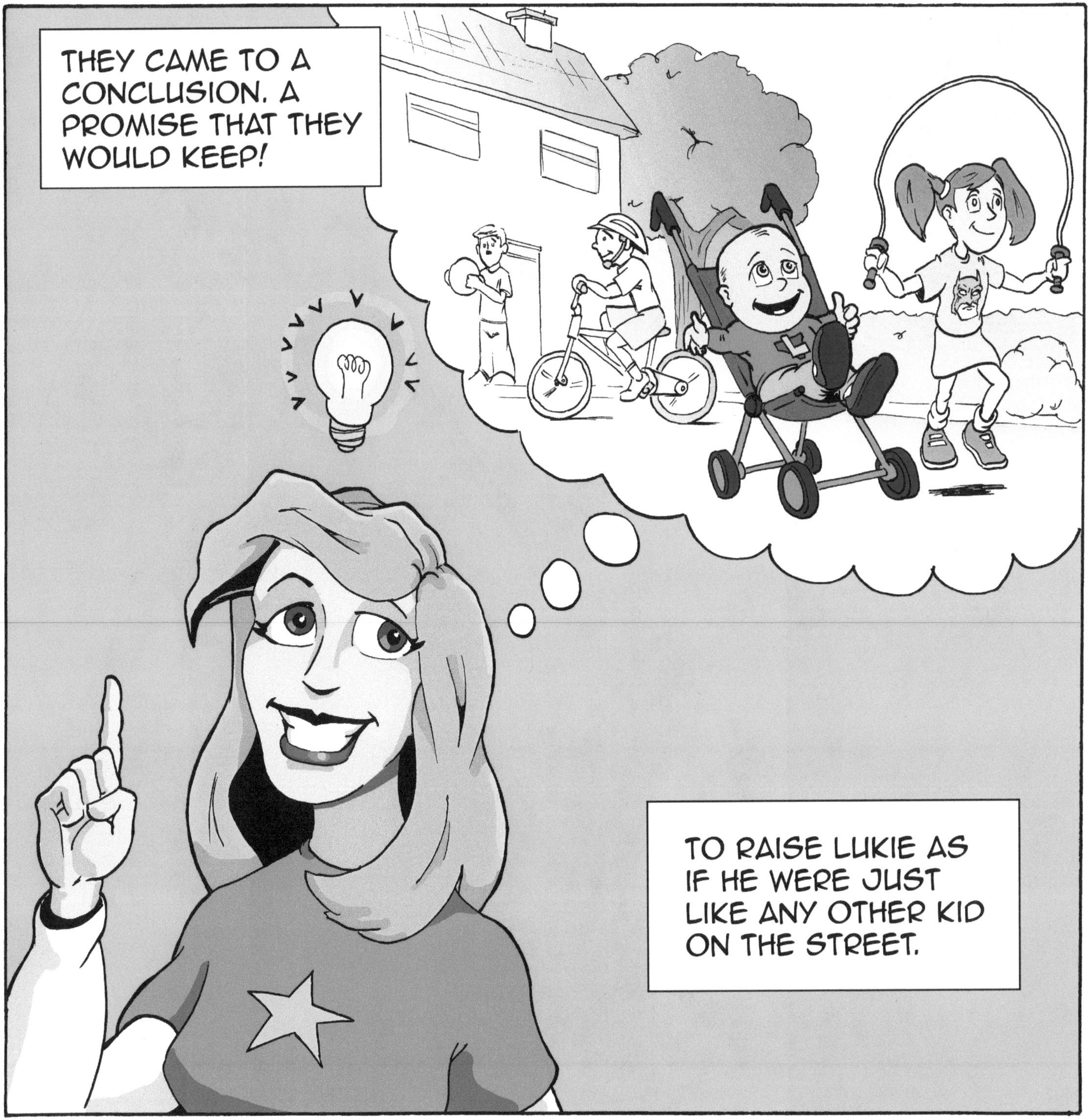
THEY CAME TO A CONCLUSION. A PROMISE THAT THEY WOULD KEEP!
TO RAISE LUKIE AS IF HE WERE JUST LIKE ANY OTHER KID ON THE STREET.

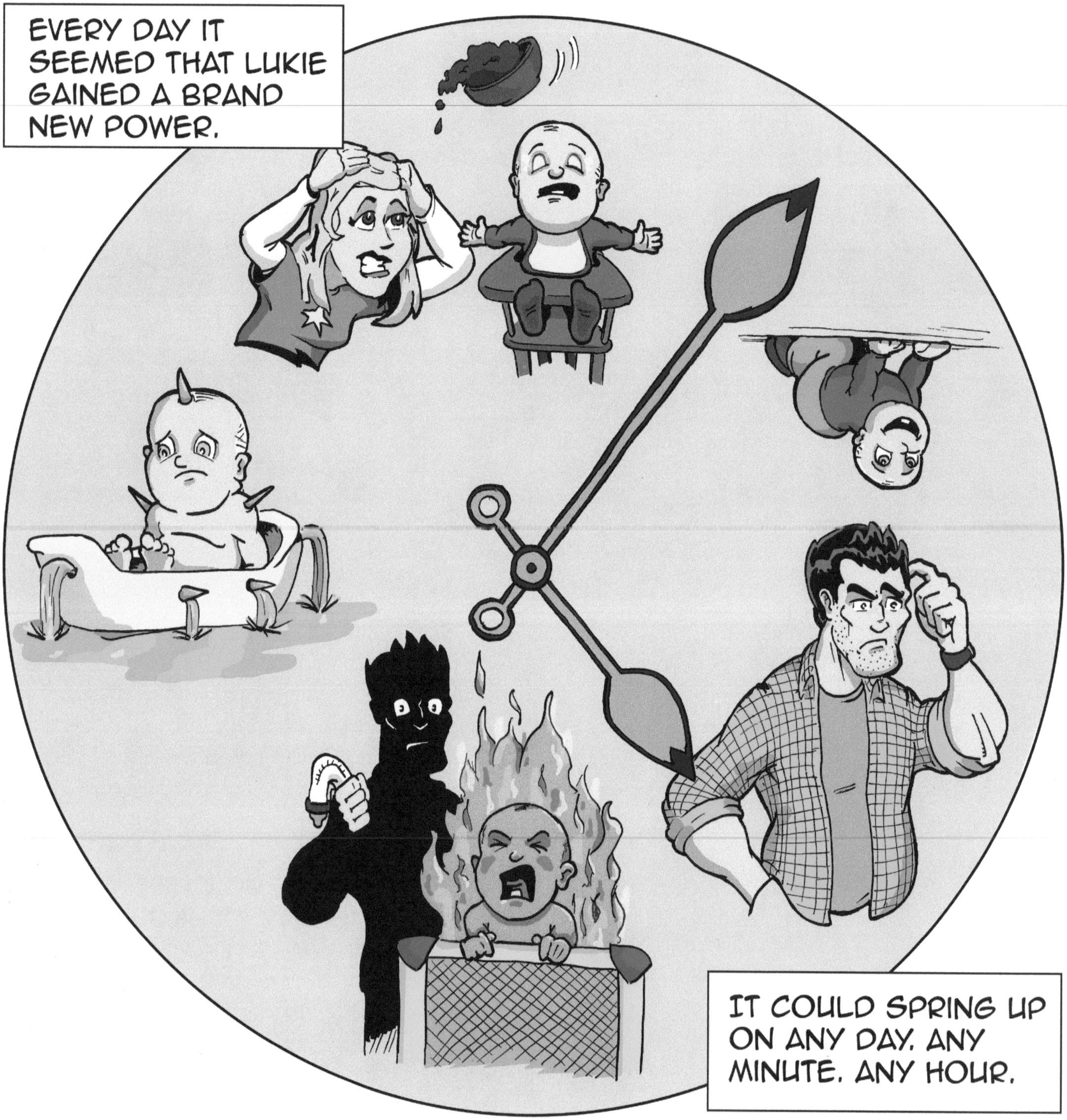
EVERY DAY IT SEEMED THAT LUKIE GAINED A BRAND NEW POWER.
IT COULD SPRING UP ON ANY DAY. ANY MINUTE. ANY HOUR.

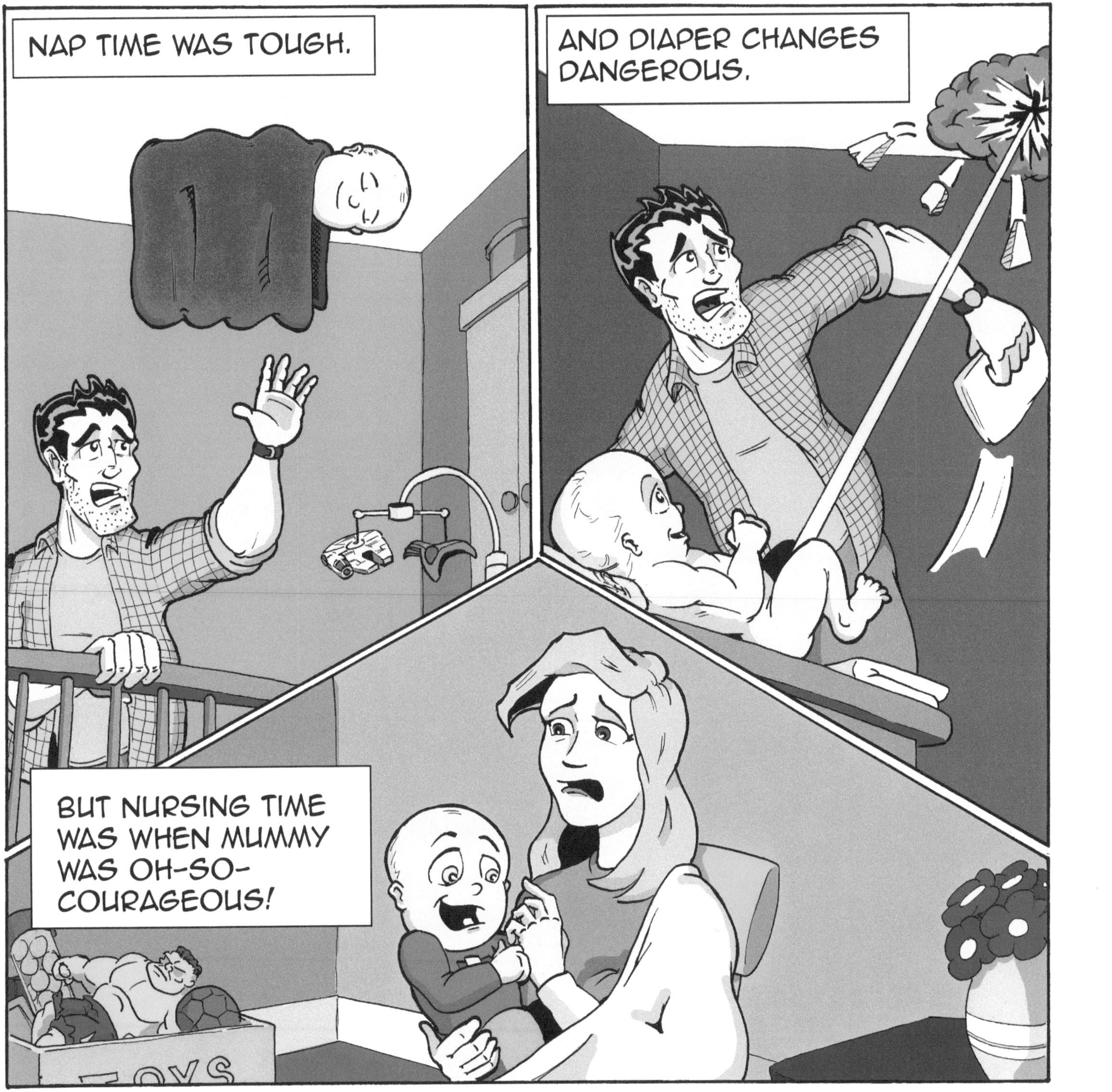
NAP TIME WAS TOUGH.
AND DIAPER CHANGES DANGEROUS.
BUT NURSING TIME WAS WHEN MUMMY WAS OH-SO-COURAGEOUS!

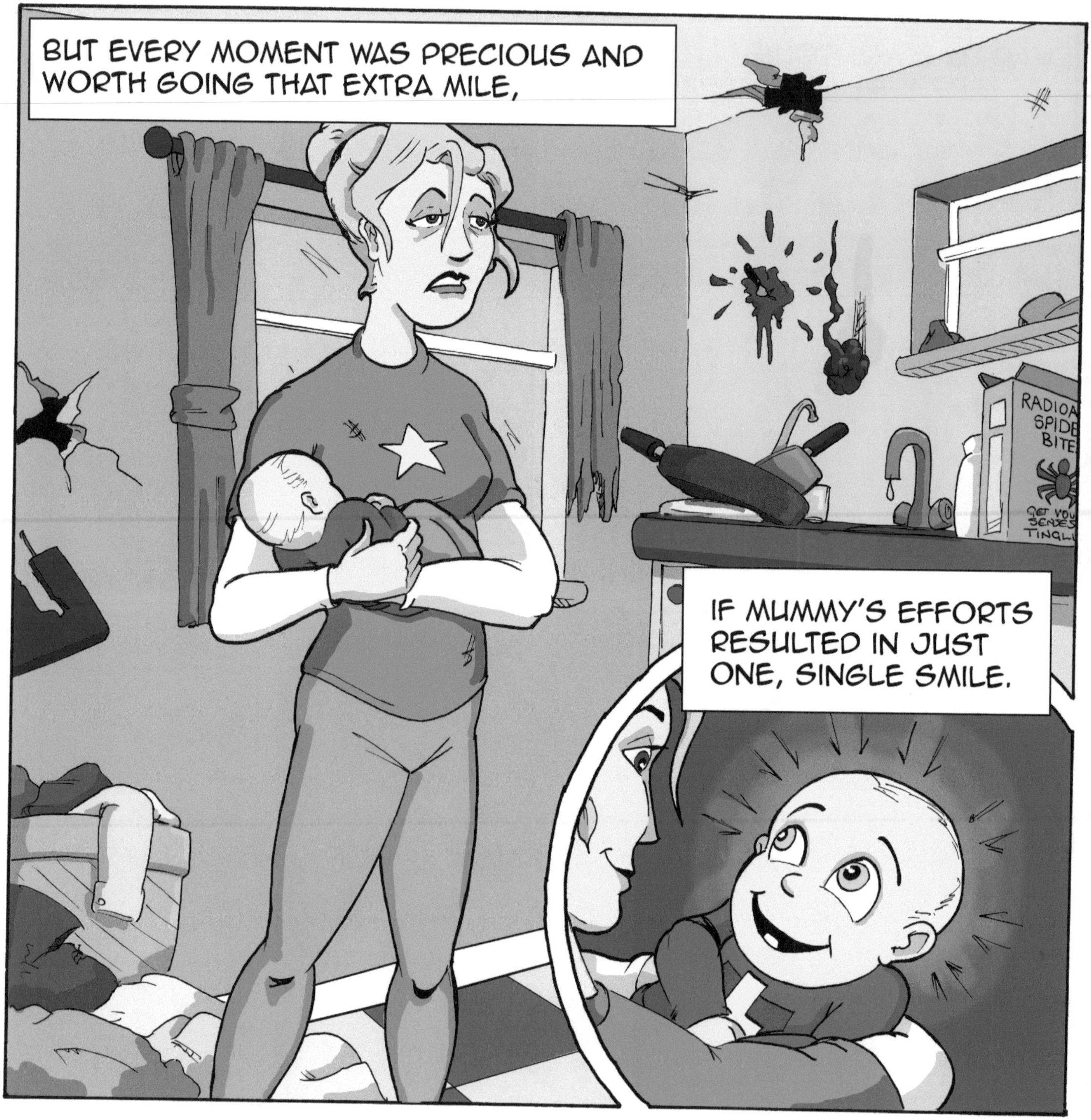
BUT EVERY MOMENT WAS PRECIOUS AND WORTH GOING THAT EXTRA MILE,
IF MUMMY'S EFFORTS RESULTED IN JUST ONE, SINGLE SMILE.

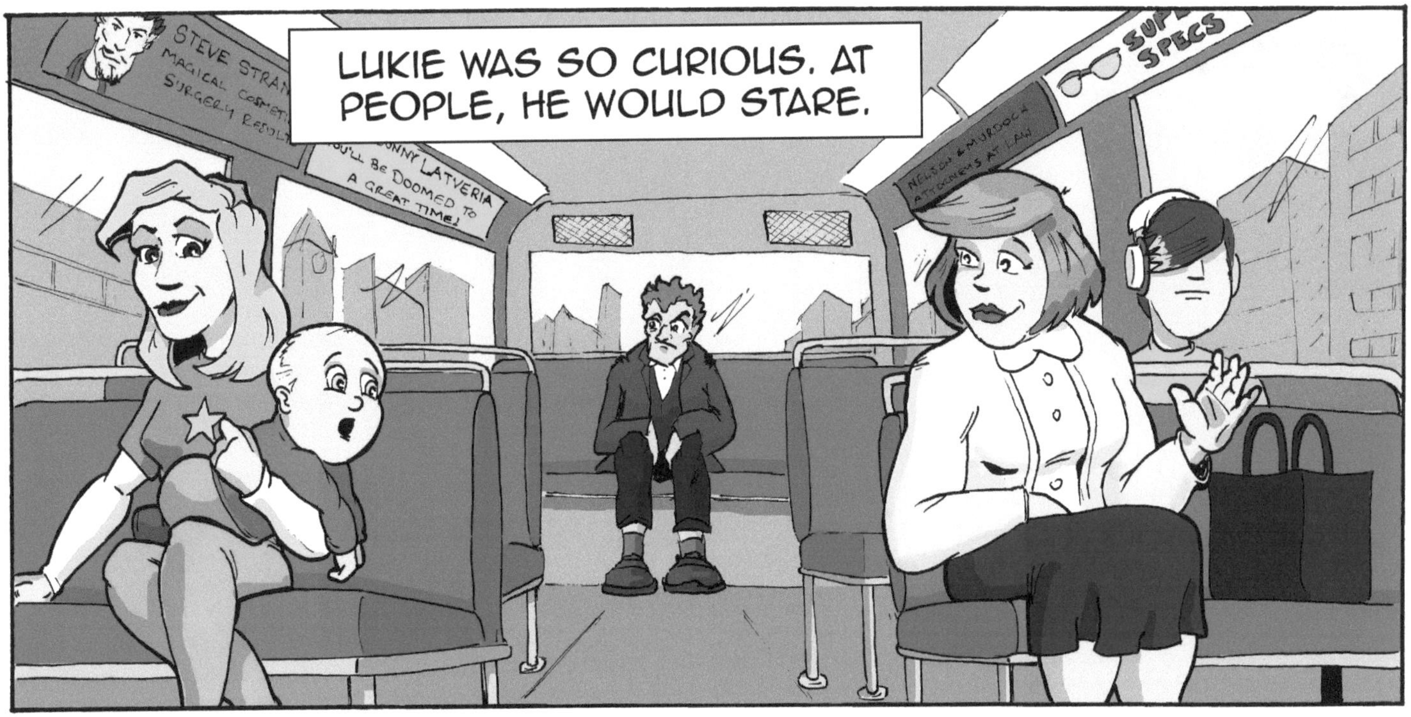
LUKIE WAS SO CURIOUS. AT PEOPLE, HE WOULD STARE.
SUNNY LATVERIA YOU'LL BE DOOMED TO A GREAT TIME!
NELSON & MURDOCK ATTORNEYS AT LAW

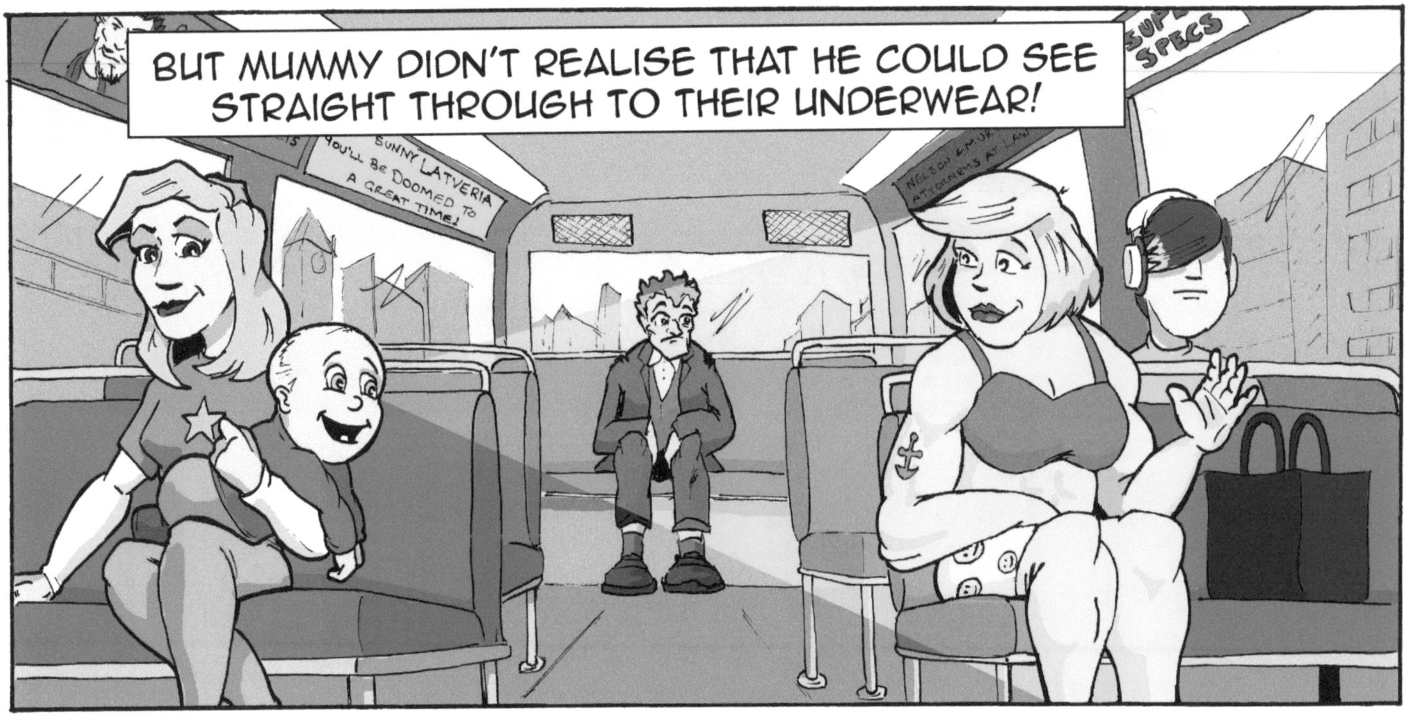
BUT MUMMY DIDN'T REALISE THAT HE COULD SEE STRAIGHT THROUGH TO THEIR UNDERWEAR!
SUNNY LATVERIA YOU'LL BE DOOMED TO A GREAT TIME!

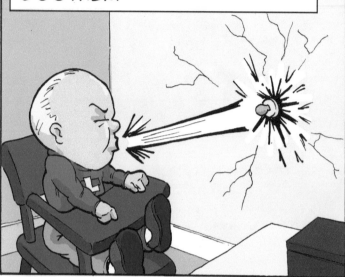

HE HAS NO INTEREST IN THE SOOTHER.

TEETHING RINGS CAN GO AWAY.

BUT ONE RATTLE OF DADDY'S HOUSE KEYS WOULD GET HIM EXCITED WITHOUT DELAY.

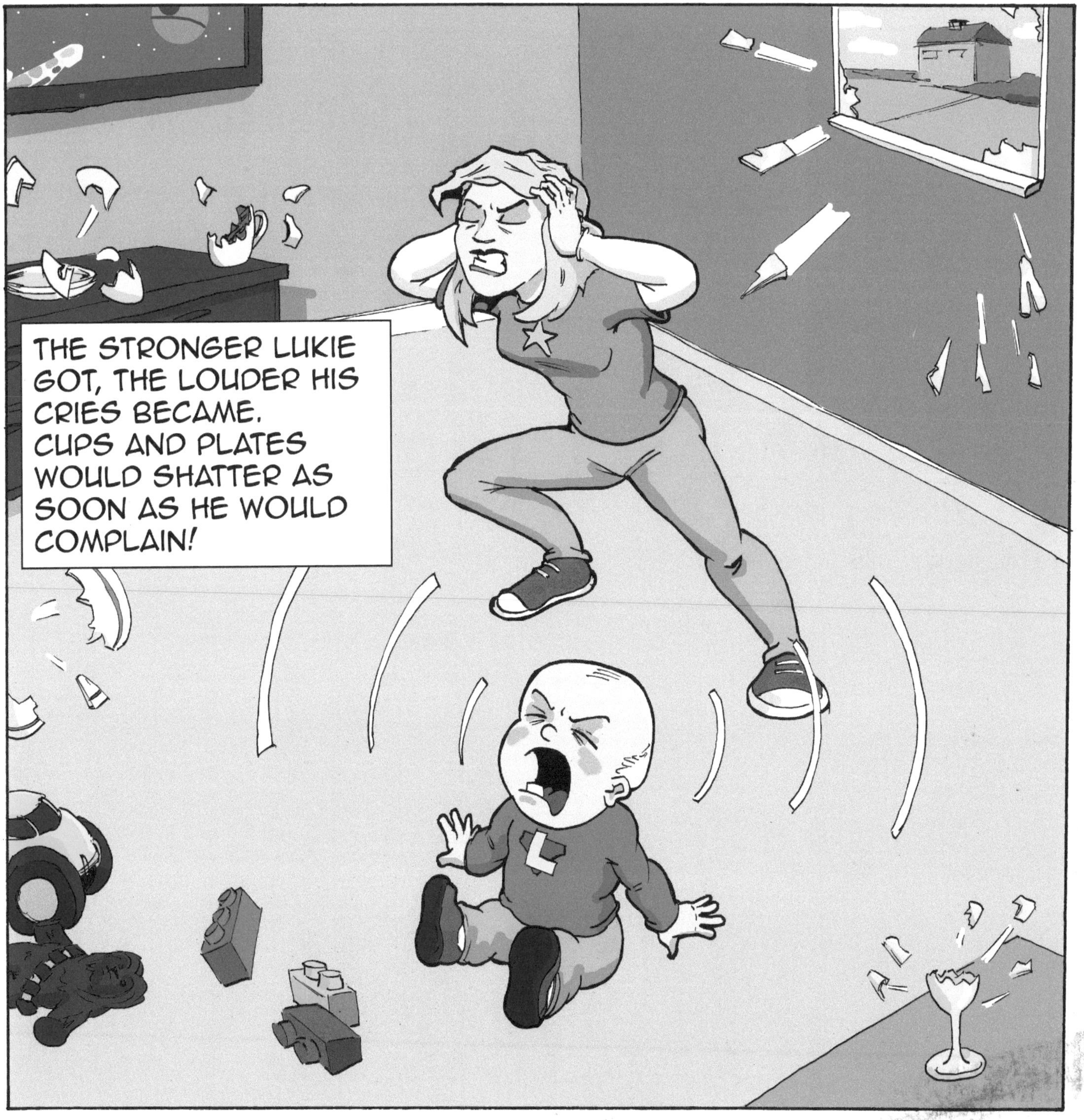
THE STRONGER LUKIE GOT, THE LOUDER HIS CRIES BECAME. CUPS AND PLATES WOULD SHATTER AS SOON AS HE WOULD COMPLAIN!

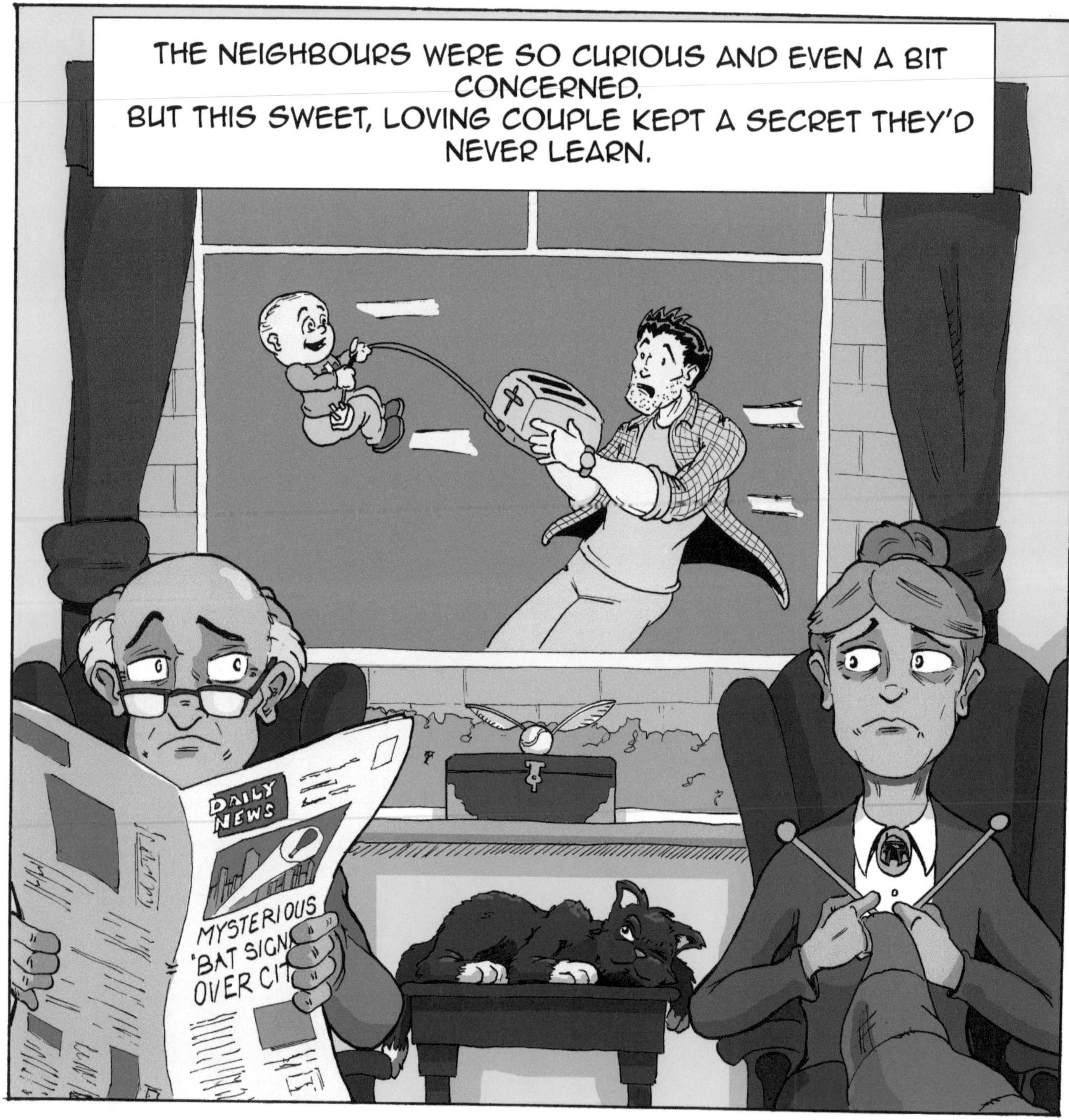
THE NEIGHBOURS WERE SO CURIOUS AND EVEN A BIT CONCERNED.
BUT THIS SWEET, LOVING COUPLE KEPT A SECRET THEY'D NEVER LEARN.
DAILY NEWS
MYSTERIOUS
'BAT SIGN
OVER CIT

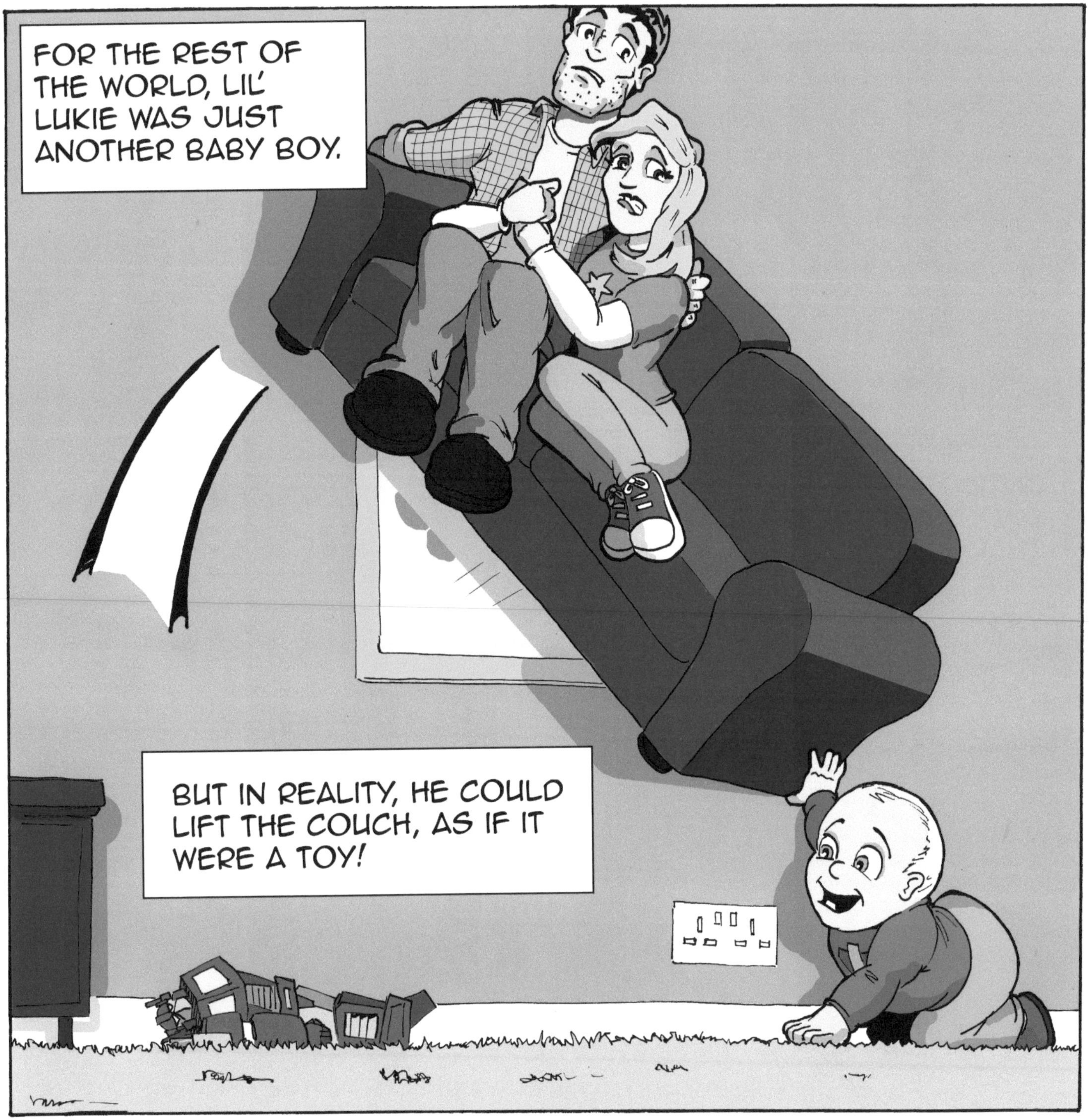
FOR THE REST OF THE WORLD, LIL' LUKIE WAS JUST ANOTHER BABY BOY.
BUT IN REALITY, HE COULD LIFT THE COUCH, AS IF IT WERE A TOY!

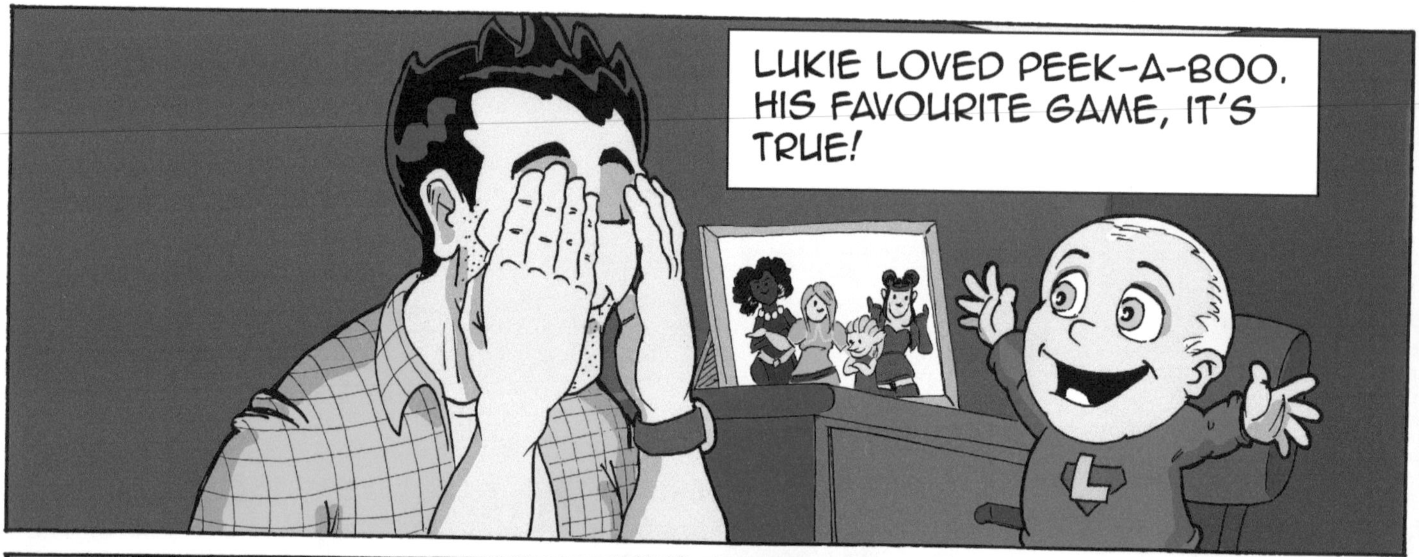
LUKIE LOVED PEEK-A-BOO. HIS FAVOURITE GAME, IT'S TRUE!

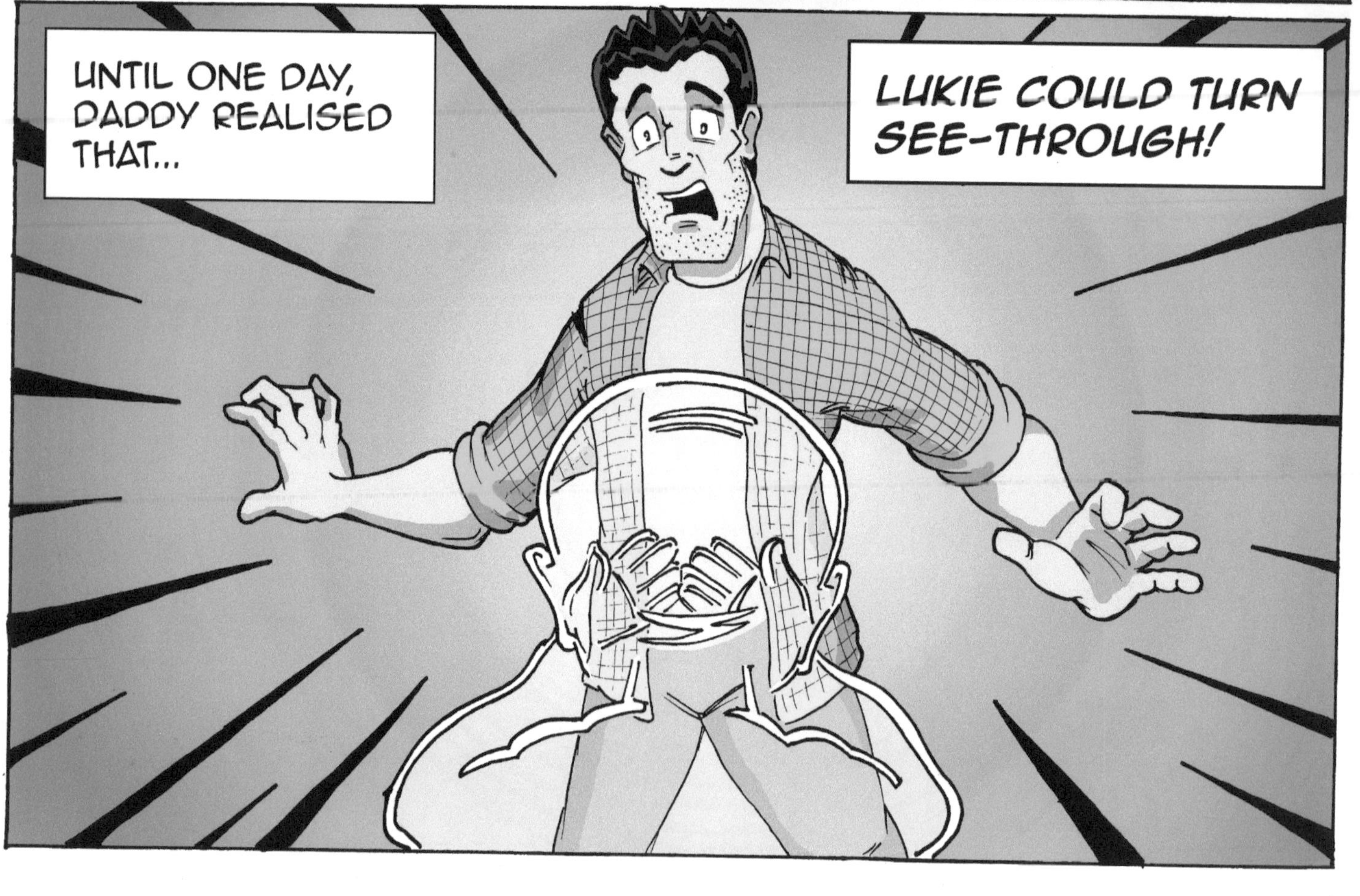
UNTIL ONE DAY, DADDY REALISED THAT...
LUKIE COULD TURN SEE-THROUGH!

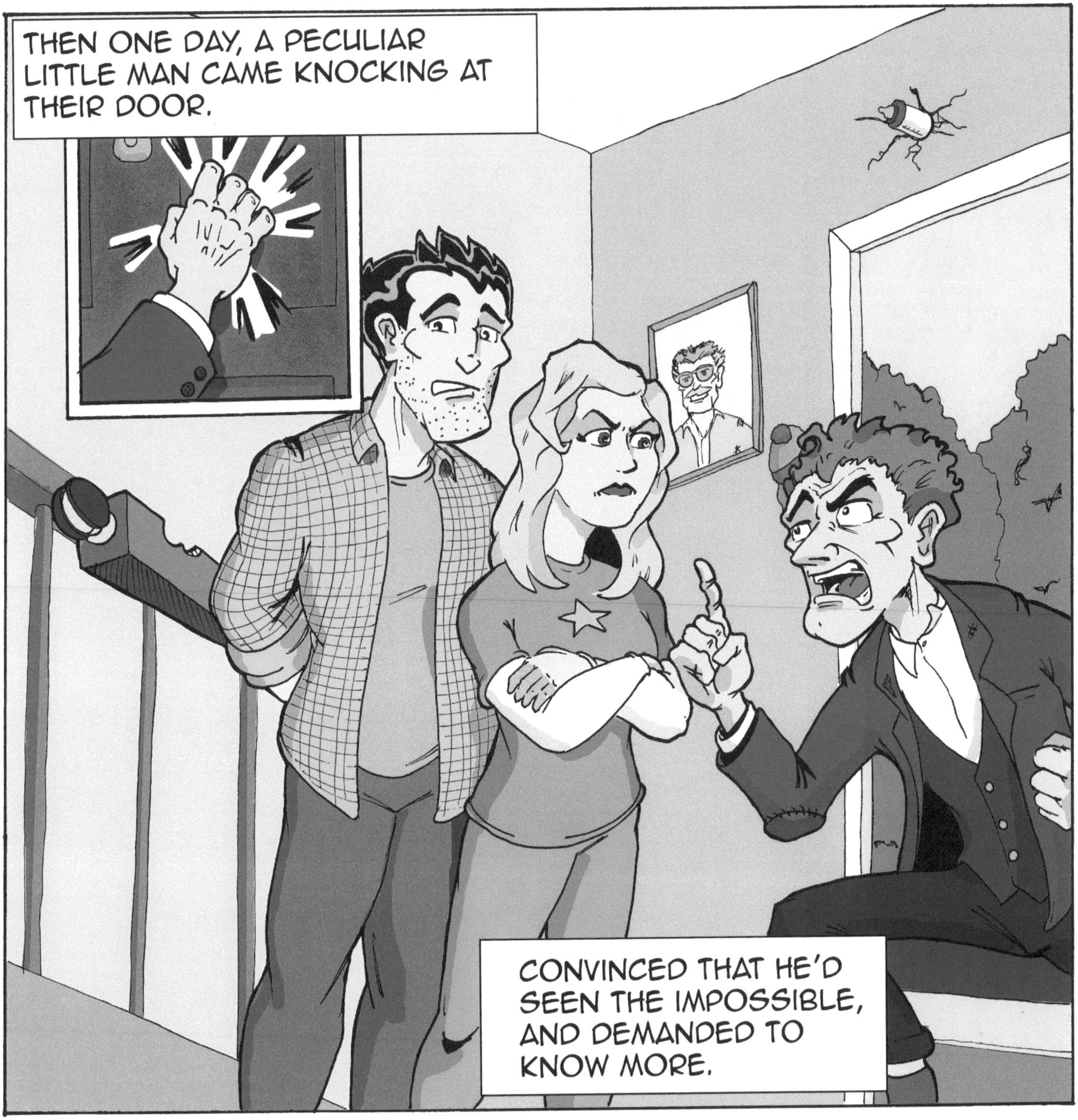
THEN ONE DAY, A PECULIAR LITTLE MAN CAME KNOCKING AT THEIR DOOR.
CONVINCED THAT HE'D SEEN THE IMPOSSIBLE, AND DEMANDED TO KNOW MORE.

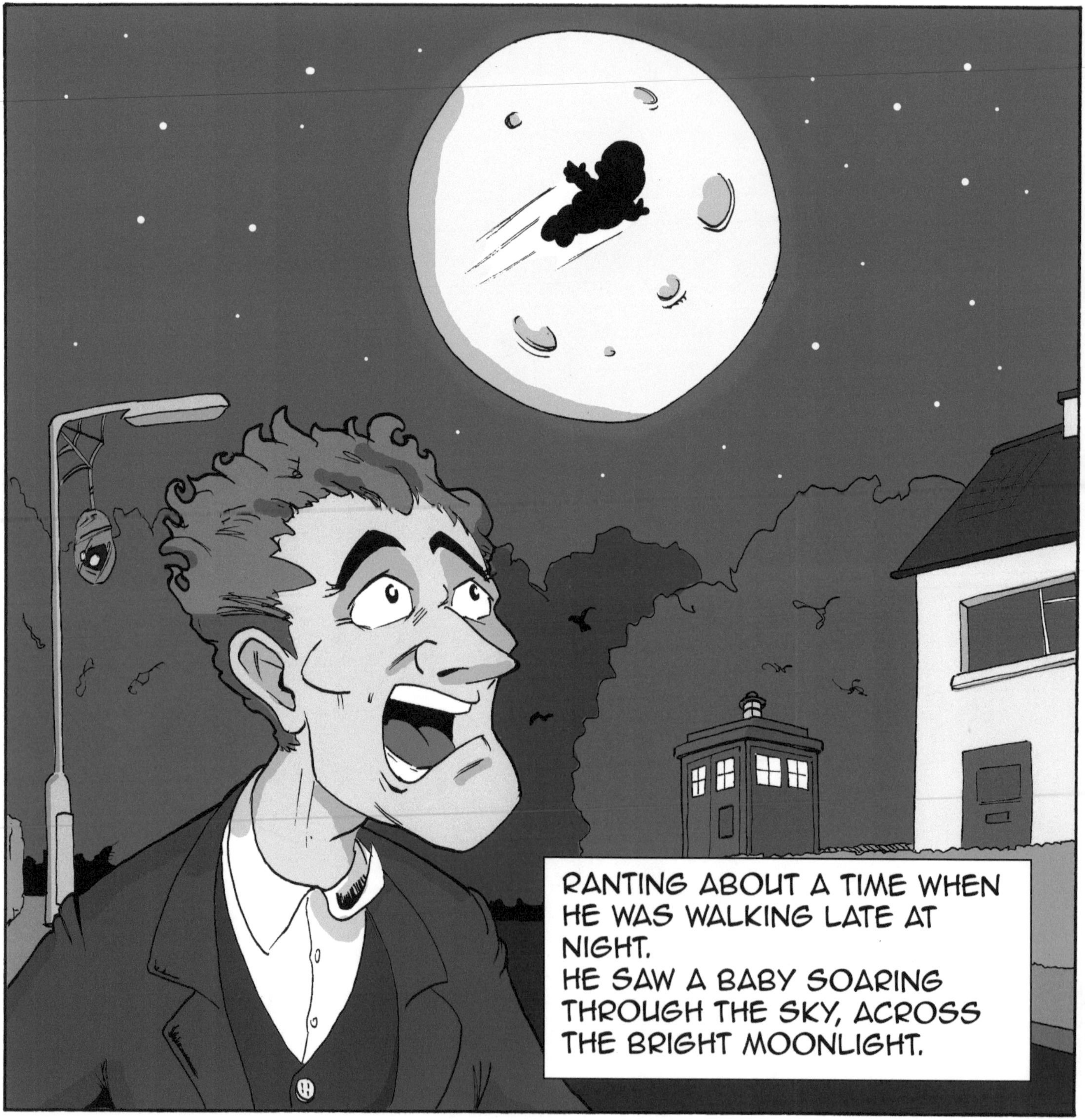
RANTING ABOUT A TIME WHEN HE WAS WALKING LATE AT NIGHT.
HE SAW A BABY SOARING THROUGH THE SKY, ACROSS THE BRIGHT MOONLIGHT.

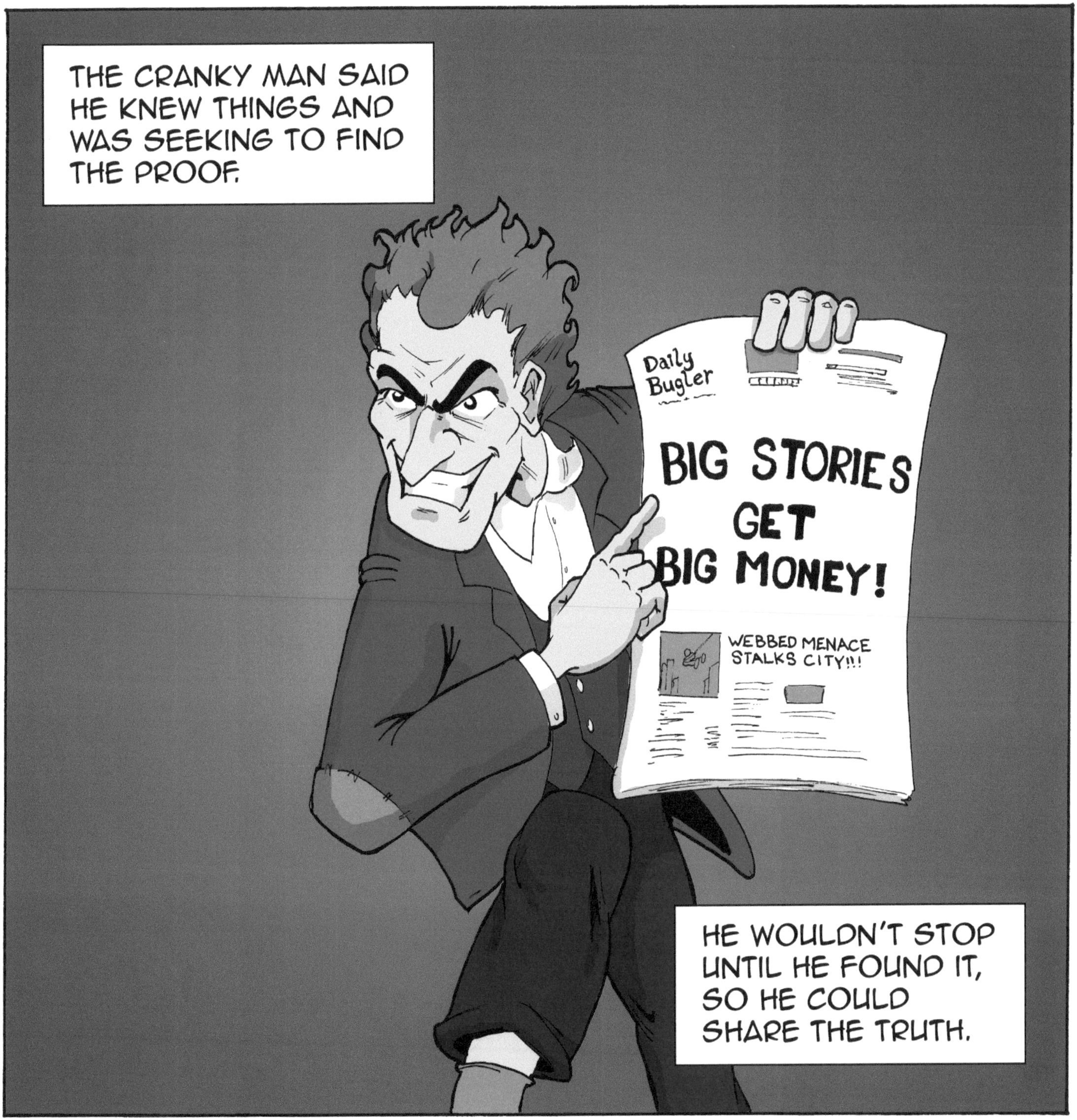
THE CRANKY MAN SAID HE KNEW THINGS AND WAS SEEKING TO FIND THE PROOF.
Daily Bugler
BIG STORIES GET BIG MONEY!
WEBBED MENACE STALKS CITY!!!
HE WOULDN'T STOP UNTIL HE FOUND IT, SO HE COULD SHARE THE TRUTH.

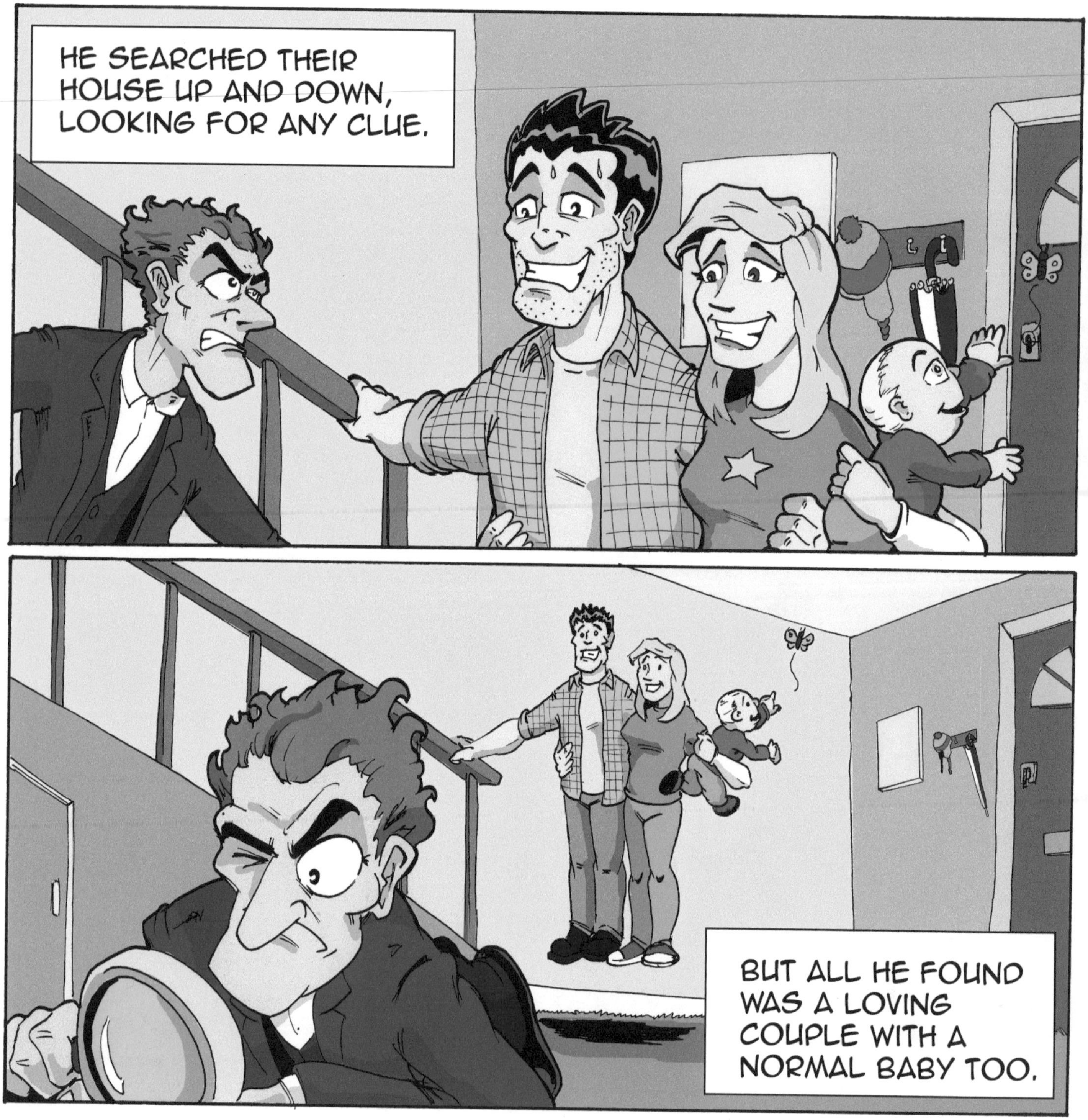
HE SEARCHED THEIR HOUSE UP AND DOWN, LOOKING FOR ANY CLUE.
BUT ALL HE FOUND WAS A LOVING COUPLE WITH A NORMAL BABY TOO.

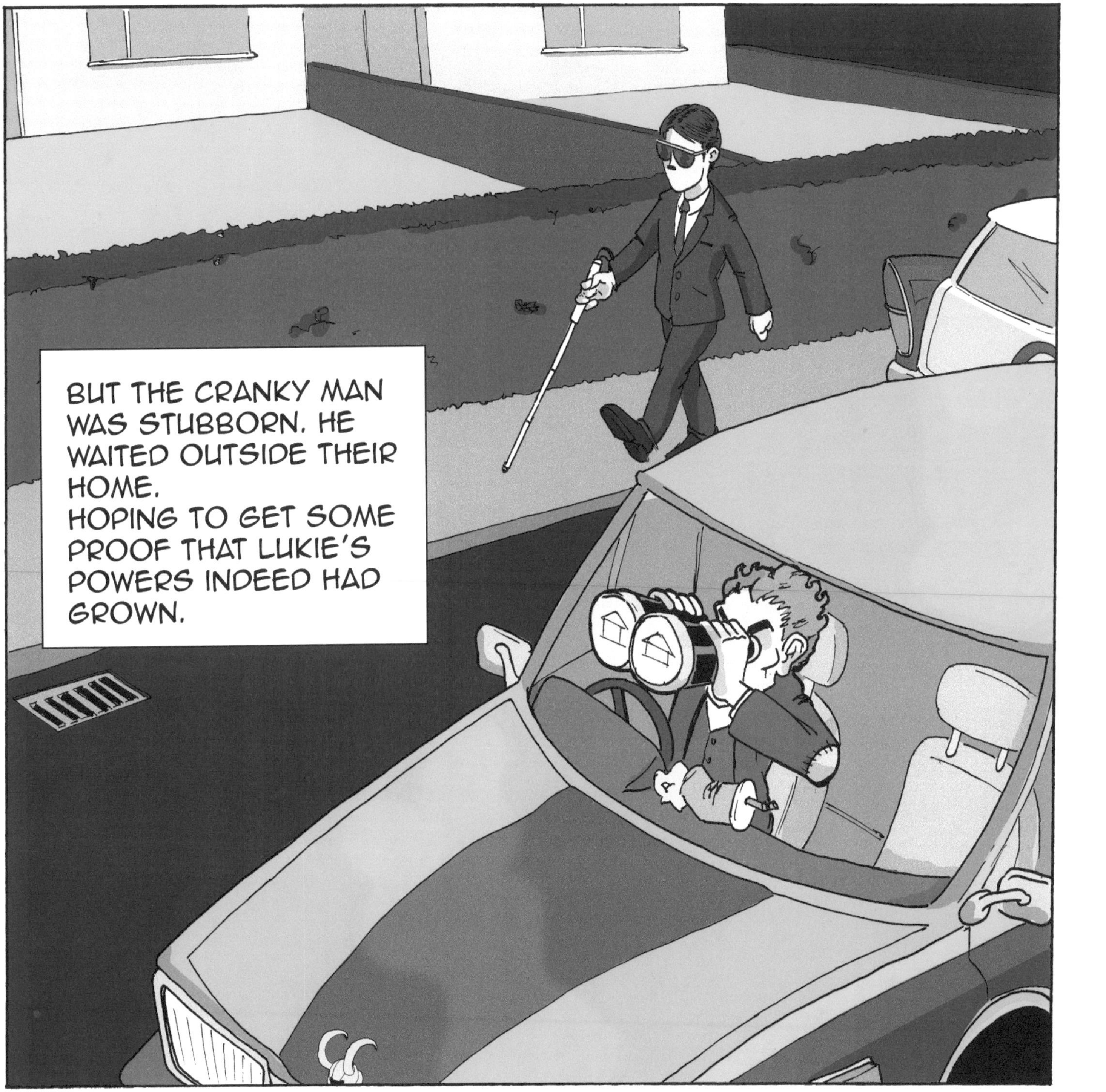
BUT THE CRANKY MAN WAS STUBBORN. HE WAITED OUTSIDE THEIR HOME.
HOPING TO GET SOME PROOF THAT LUKIE'S POWERS INDEED HAD GROWN.

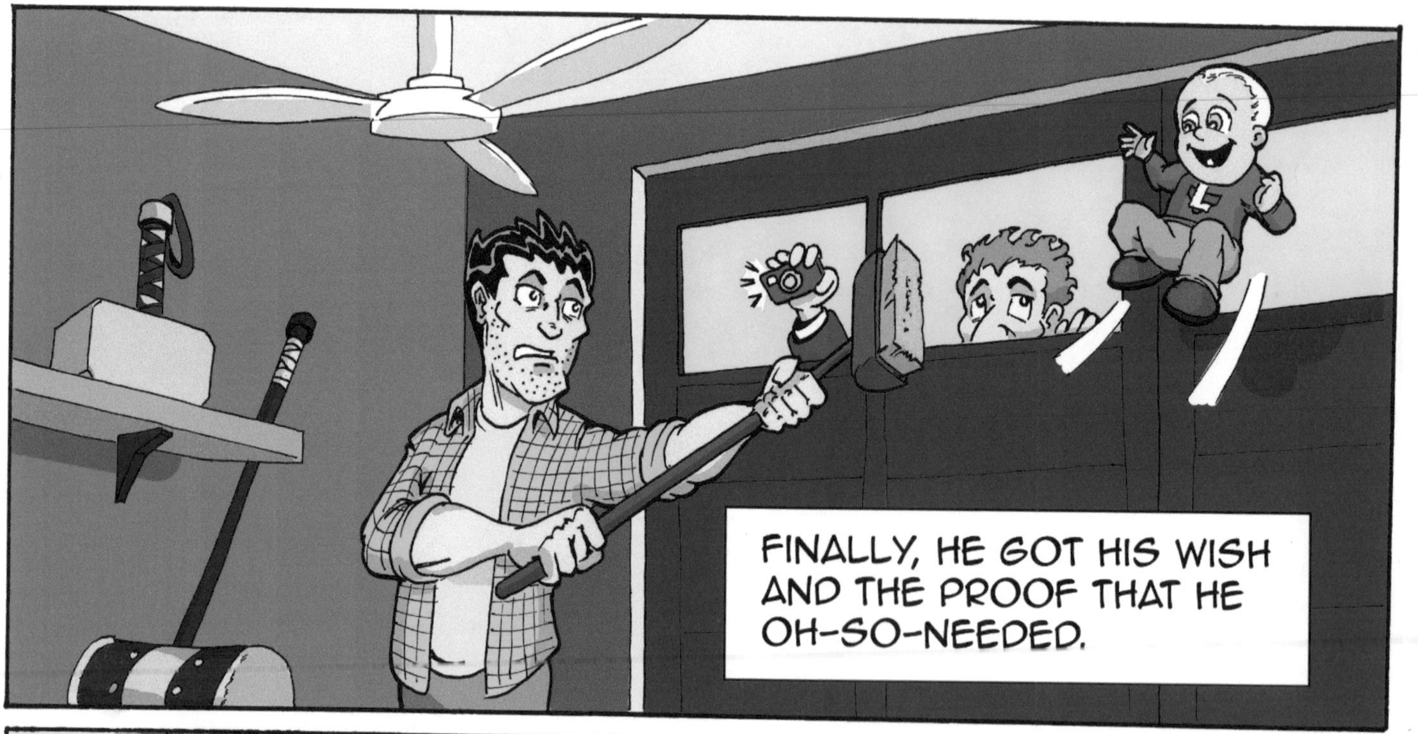
FINALLY, HE GOT HIS WISH AND THE PROOF THAT HE OH-SO-NEEDED.

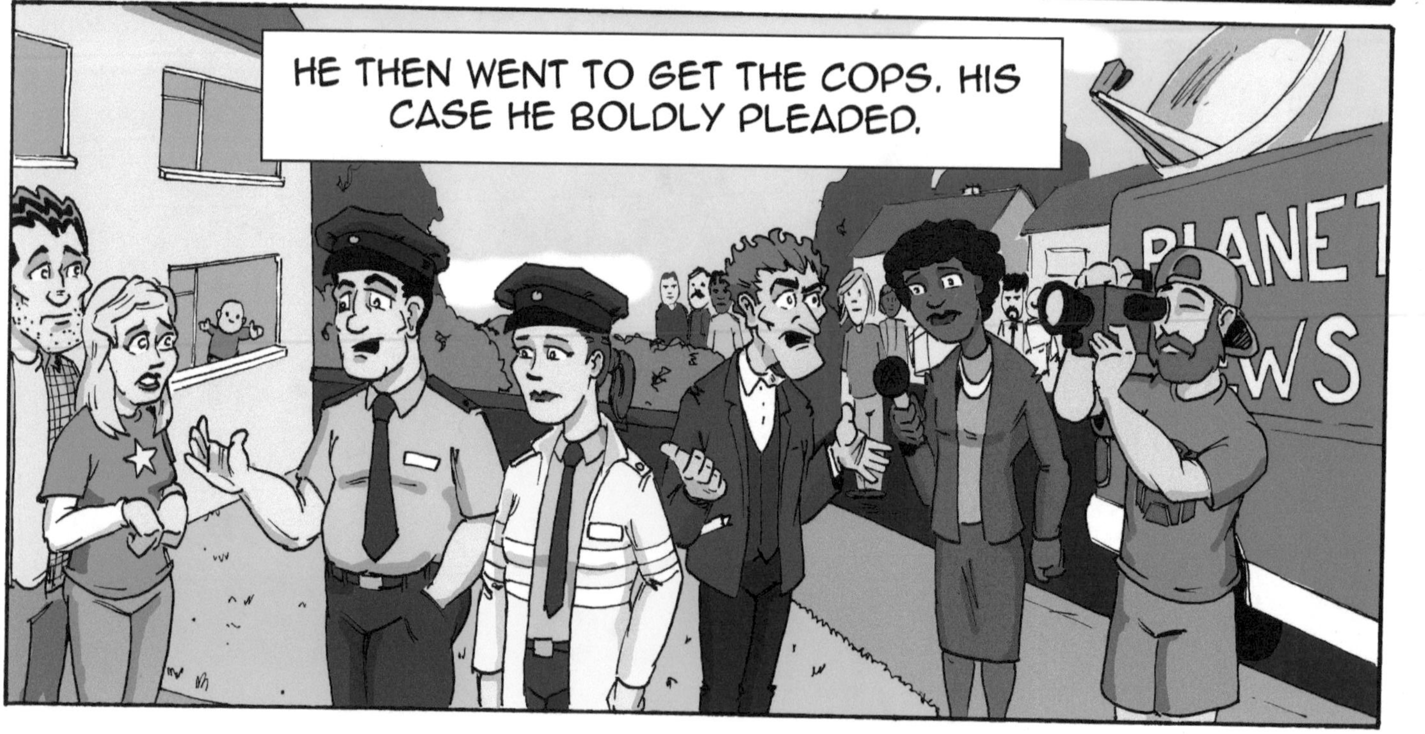
HE THEN WENT TO GET THE COPS. HIS CASE HE BOLDLY PLEADED.
PLANET
EWS

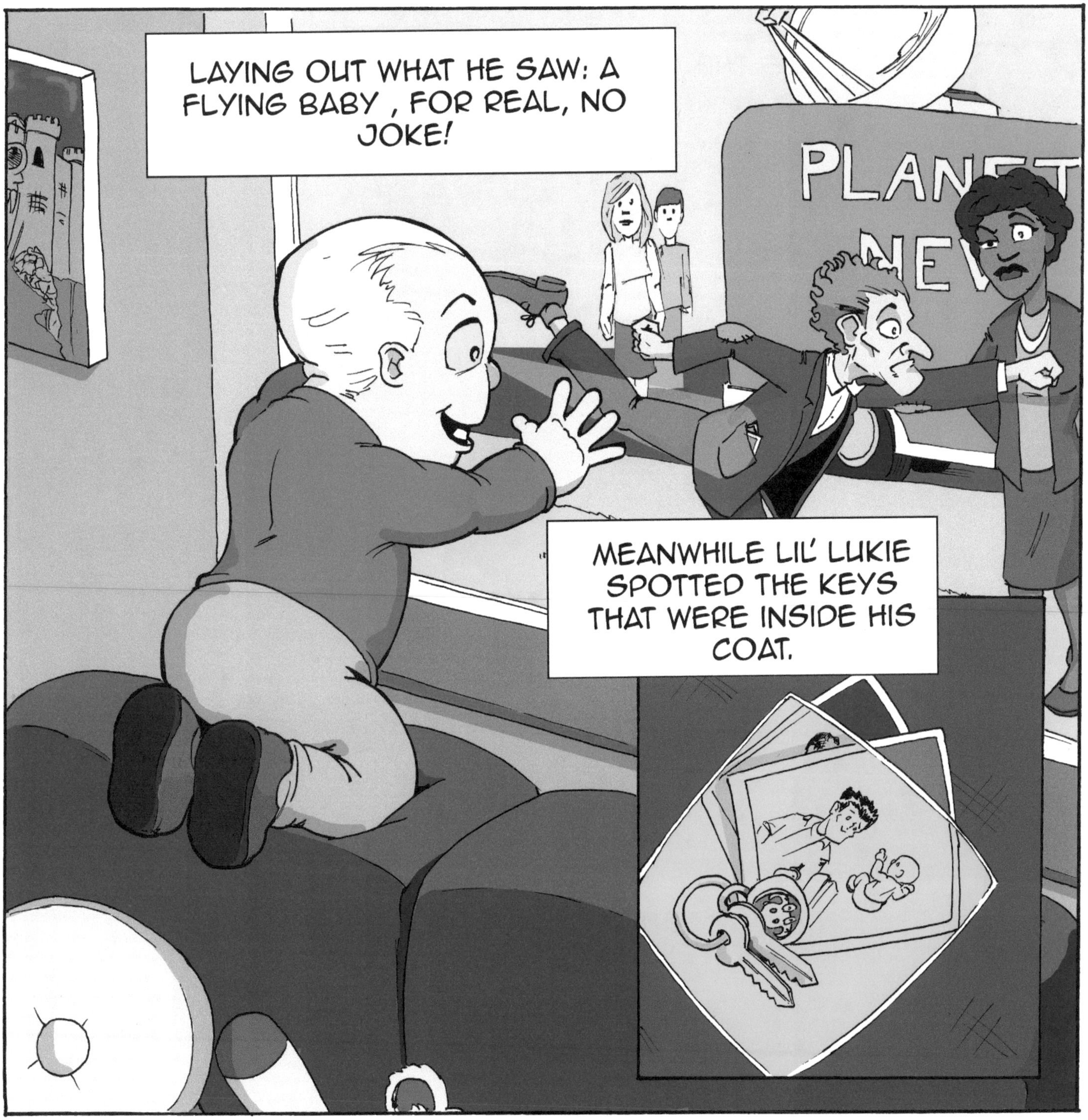
LAYING OUT WHAT HE SAW: A FLYING BABY , FOR REAL, NO JOKE!
PLANET NEW
MEANWHILE LIL' LUKIE SPOTTED THE KEYS THAT WERE INSIDE HIS COAT.

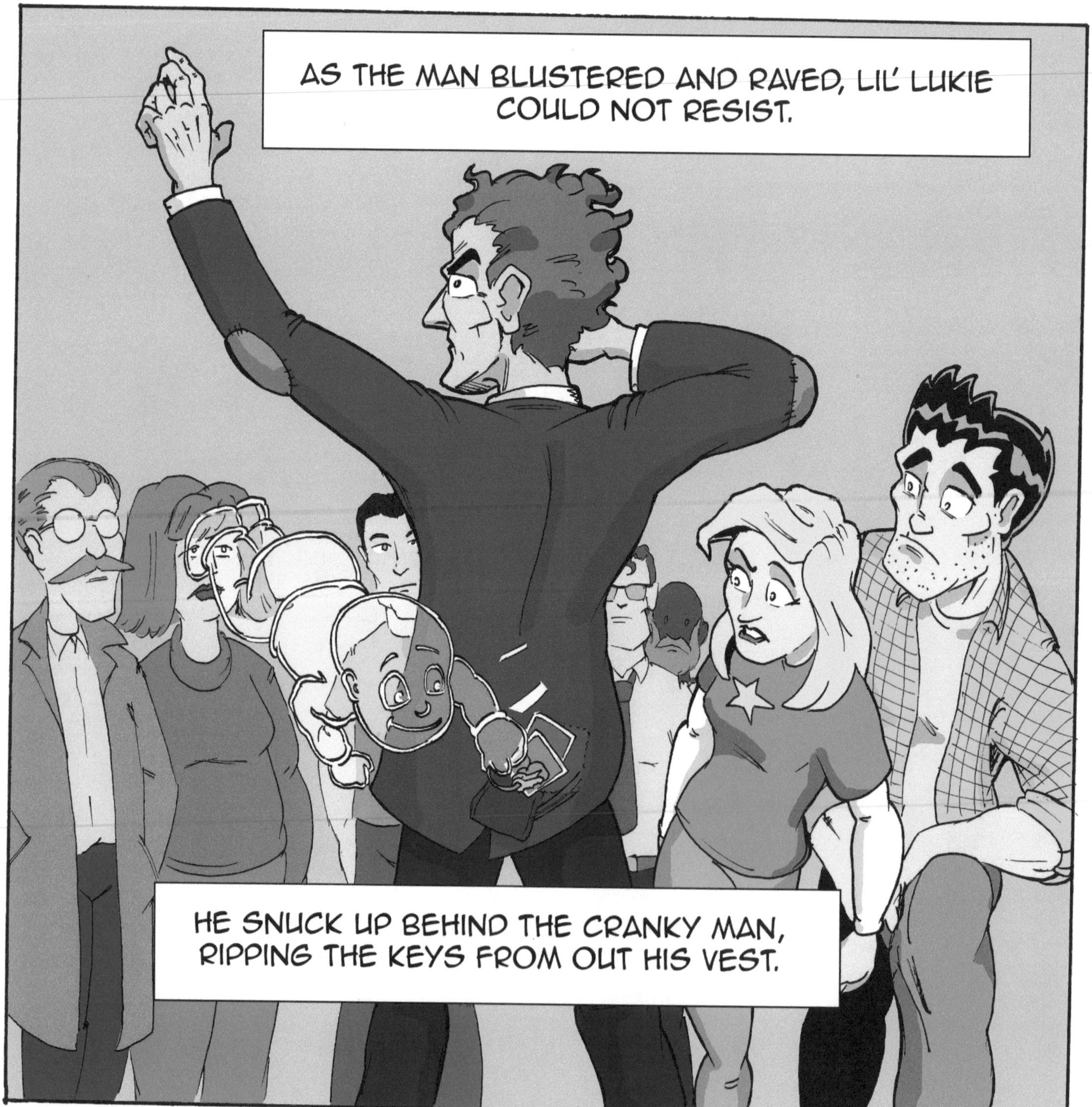
AS THE MAN BLUSTERED AND RAVED, LIL' LUKIE COULD NOT RESIST.
HE SNUCK UP BEHIND THE CRANKY MAN, RIPPING THE KEYS FROM OUT HIS VEST.

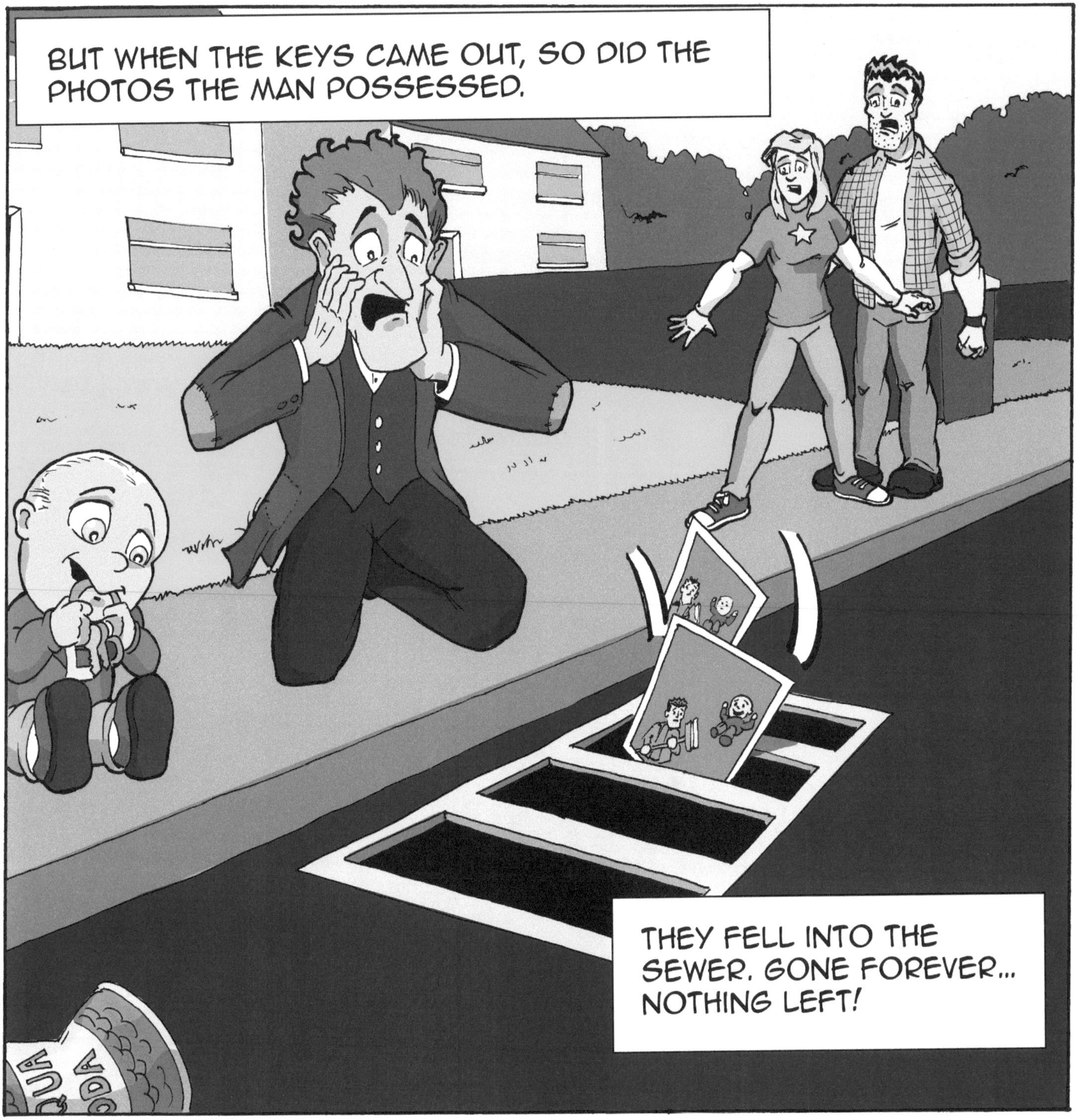
BUT WHEN THE KEYS CAME OUT, SO DID THE PHOTOS THE MAN POSSESSED.
THEY FELL INTO THE SEWER. GONE FOREVER... NOTHING LEFT!

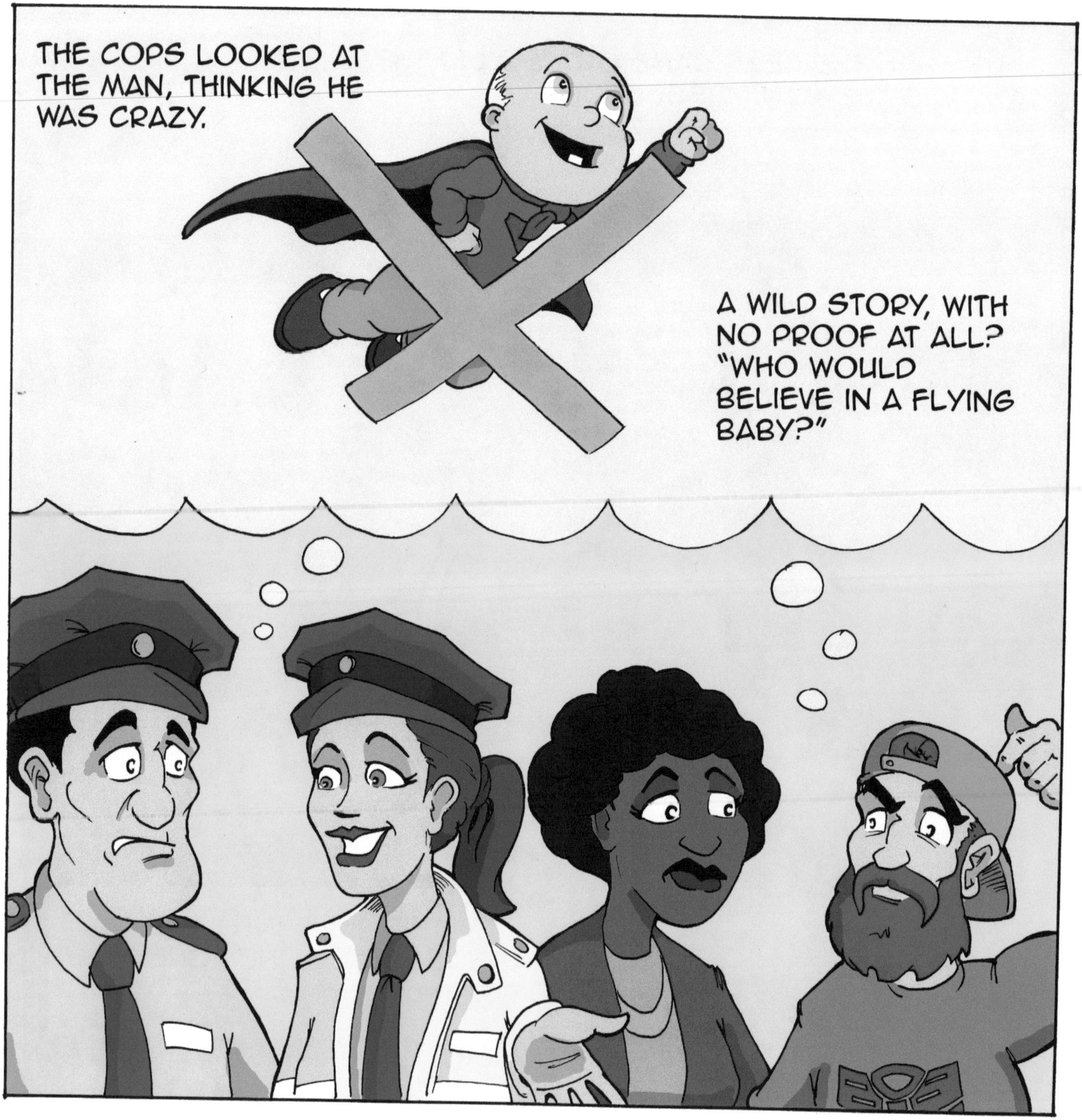
THE COPS LOOKED AT THE MAN, THINKING HE WAS CRAZY.
A WILD STORY, WITH NO PROOF AT ALL? "WHO WOULD BELIEVE IN A FLYING BABY?"

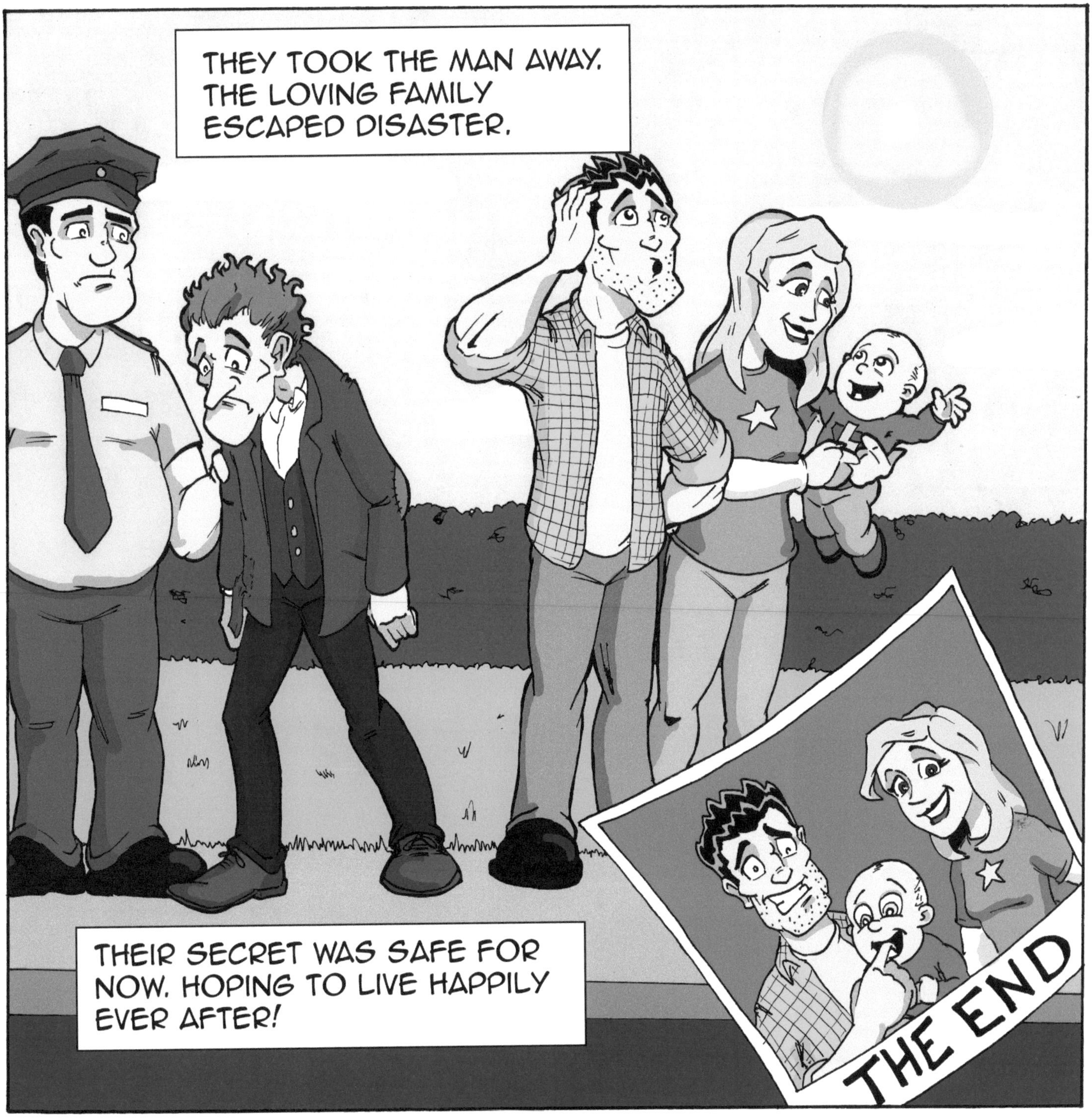
THEY TOOK THE MAN AWAY. THE LOVING FAMILY ESCAPED DISASTER.
THEIR SECRET WAS SAFE FOR NOW. HOPING TO LIVE HAPPILY EVER AFTER!
THE END

LIL' LUKIE
WILL RETURN...